Dear Parents and Educators,

Welcome to Penguin Young Readers! As parents and educators, you know that each child develops at his or her own pace—in terms of speech, critical thinking, and, of course, reading. Penguin Young Readers recognizes this fact. As a result, each Penguin Young Readers book is assigned a traditional easy-to-read level (1–4) as well as a Guided Reading Level (A–P). Both of these systems will help you choose the right book for your child. Please refer to the back of each book for specific leveling information. Penguin Young Readers features esteemed authors and illustrators, stories about favorite characters, fascinating nonfiction, and more!

Mo Jackson: Pass the Ball, Mo!

LEVEL **2**

GUIDED READING LEVEL **I**

This book is perfect for a **Progressing Reader** who:
- can figure out unknown words by using picture and context clues;
- can recognize beginning, middle, and ending sounds;
- can make and confirm predictions about what will happen in the text; and
- can distinguish between fiction and nonfiction.

Here are some **activities** you can do during and after reading this book:
- Picture Clues: Use the pictures to tell the story. Have the child go through the book, retelling the story just by looking at the pictures.
- Sight Words: Sight words are frequently used words that readers must know just by looking at them. They are known instantly, on sight. Knowing these words helps children develop into efficient readers. As you read the story, have the child point out the sight words below.

after	from	his	of	take
by	him	into	over	with

Remember, sharing the love of reading with a child is the best gift you can give!

—Sarah Fabiny, Editorial Director
   Penguin Young Readers program

*Penguin Young Readers are leveled by independent reviewers applying the standards developed by Irene Fountas and Gay Su Pinnell in *Matching Books to Readers: Using Leveled Books in Guided Reading*, Heinemann, 1999.

For my great-niece Avigail Felice—DAA

For Paul—SR

PENGUIN YOUNG READERS
An Imprint of Penguin Random House LLC

Penguin supports copyright. Copyright fuels creativity, encourages diverse voices,
promotes free speech, and creates a vibrant culture. Thank you for buying an authorized edition
of this book and for complying with copyright laws by not reproducing, scanning, or distributing any
part of it in any form without permission. You are supporting writers and allowing Penguin to
continue to publish books for every reader.

Text copyright © 2018 by David Adler. Illustrations copyright © 2018 by Sam Ricks. All rights reserved.
Previously published in hardcover in 2018 by Penguin Young Readers. This paperback edition published
in 2019 by Penguin Young Readers, an imprint of Penguin Random House LLC, 345 Hudson Street,
New York, New York 10014. Manufactured in China.

The Library of Congress has catalogued the hardcover edition
under the following Control Number: 2018285559

ISBN 9780425289808   10 9 8 7 6 5

PASS THE BALL, MO!

by David A. Adler
illustrated by Sam Ricks

Penguin Young Readers
An Imprint of Penguin Random House

"Who was our first president?"

Mo Jackson's teacher asks.

"George Basketball," Mo says.

Mo's teacher shakes his head.

"His name was George Washington,

not George Basketball."

"Oh," Mo says.

He's not thinking about presidents.

He's thinking about
basketball practice.

It's right after school.

At practice Coach Emma says,

"Mo, pass the ball."

Mo passes it to Gail.

It hits her knee and

bounces away.

"No, no!" Coach Emma says.

"Gail is taller than you.

Throw higher."

Everyone on the team

is taller than Mo.

Mo's team is the Bees.

Mo practices passing.

He throws the ball

against the wall.

"Throw it higher,"

Coach Emma tells him.

Mo throws the ball higher.

Coach Emma blows a whistle.

Tweet! Tweet!

Practice is done.

The Bees' first game is Saturday.

Mo walks home with his dad.

"I have to practice passing,"

he tells his dad.

Mo practices with his dad.

"Pass the ball," Mo's dad says.

His dad is even taller

than Gail.

Mo throws the ball high.

"Good pass," Mo's dad says.

It's Saturday.

"Eat a big breakfast,"

Mo's mother says.

"Basketball players need

to be strong."

One by one, Mo tosses blueberries
into his bowl of cereal.

Each time a berry lands in the bowl,

Mo says, "Yeah! Two points!"

He eats his breakfast.

His mom and dad take

him to the game.

They sit in the stands and watch.

The Bees are playing the Ducks.

Mo and Eve sit on the bench

and watch.

The Bees and Ducks run
from one end of the court
to the other.

They pass the ball.

They shoot the ball.

Sometimes it goes in.

Most times it doesn't.

Tweet! Tweet!

The first half is done.

The Ducks are winning 12 to 10.

The second half starts.
Mo and Eve are still on
the bench.
"I need to rest," Sam tells
Coach Emma.
"Go in," Coach tells Eve.

The game is almost over.

The score is Ducks 18,

Bees 18.

"I need to rest," Gail tells

Coach Emma.

"Go in," Coach tells Mo.

Mo runs onto the court.

"Hey, Little One," a Duck says to Mo.

"I'm not Little One. My name is Mo."

The Duck tells Mo, "And I'm Big Max."

Mo runs up and down the court.

Big Max runs with him.

Billy shoots the ball.

It hits the rim and rebounds to Mo.

"Pass it!" Coach Emma says.

"Pass it to me!" Janet says.

"Pass it to me!" Billy says.

Big Max is in the way.

"Here goes," Mo says.

He throws the ball high

over Max's head.

It is also over Janet's head.

It's over Billy's head, too.

The ball goes in the basket!

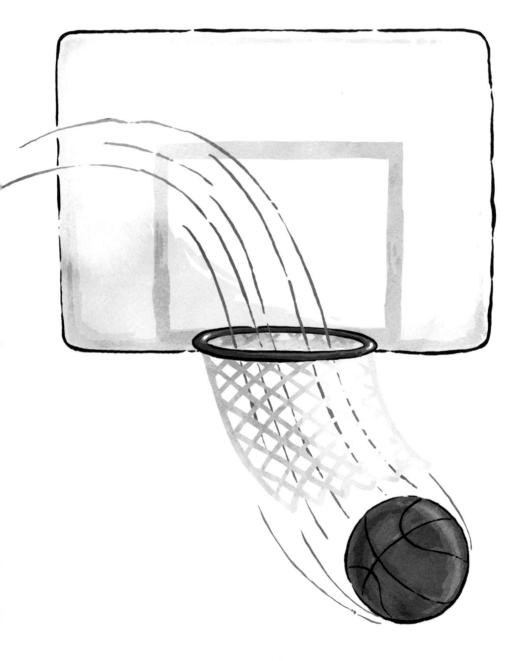

"YEAH!" Mo's parents and others cheer.

"Two points!" Coach Emma shouts.

Tweet! Tweet!

The game is over.

The Bees win 20 to 18.

The Bees carry Mo on their
shoulders.
They carry him
to his parents.

"Great shot," Mo's parents tell him.

"But I was trying to pass the ball,"

Mo says.

Coach Emma laughs.

"It was a very bad pass.

But your bad pass

won the game."